MW01034382

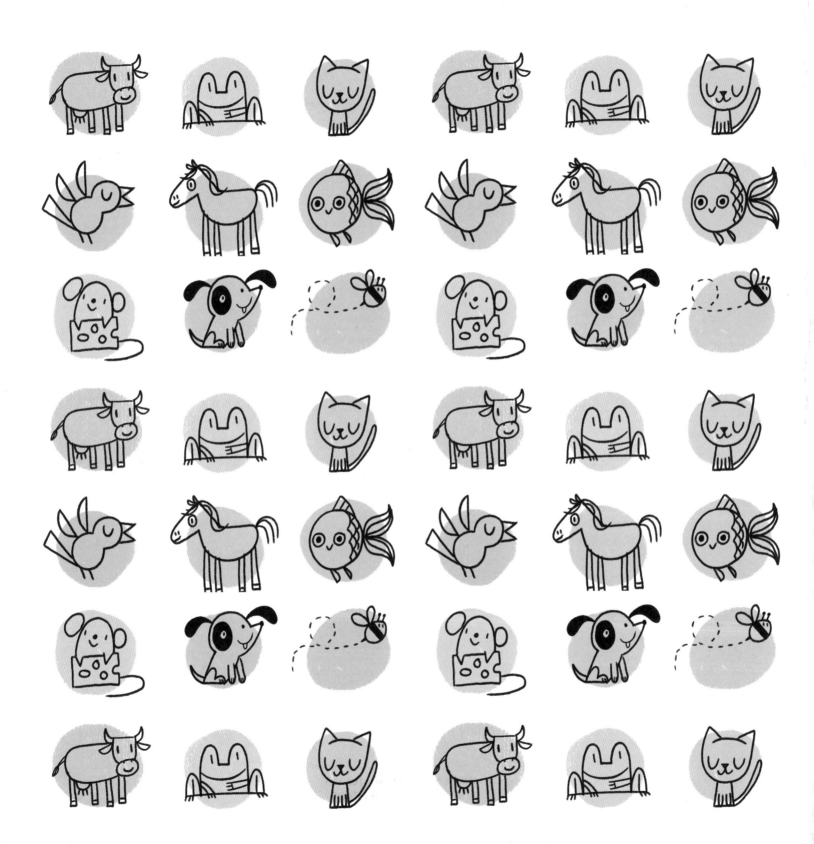

Guess Who, Haiku

Words by **Deanna Caswell** Pictures by **Bob Shea**

Abrams Appleseed

New York

Here's a haiku
just for you!

new day on the farm
muffled mooing announces
a fresh pail of milk

Can you guess who from this haiku?

A cow!

This cow has a haiku just for you.

flower visitors
busy buzzing in the field
black and yellow stripes

Can you guess who from her haiku?

A bee!

This bee has a haiku just for you.

a soft nose in oats
after an afternoon ride
back at the stable

Can you guess who from his haiku?

A horse!

This horse has a haiku just for you.

one small speckled egg
wings wrap a breezy cradle
up on the treetop

Can you guess who from her haiku?

A bird!

This bird has a haiku just for you.

from a lily pad
keen eyes spy a careless fly
a sticky tongue—SNAP!

Can you guess who from her haiku?

A frog!

This frog has a haiku just for you.

the whole wide river
in the hollow of a log
a silver tail fin

Can you guess who from his haiku?

A fish!

This fish has a haiku just for you.

a chunk of Swiss cheese
chewing sounds heard from a hole
in the kitchen wall

Can you guess who from his haiku?

A mouse!

This mouse has a haiku just for you.

full belly purring
whiskers frame milk-scented yawns
beloved stuffed pet

Can you guess who from her haiku?

A cat!

This cat has a haiku just for you.

**sitting for a treat
an eager tail smacks the ground
over and over**

Can you guess who from his haiku?

A dog!

This dog has a haiku just for you.

two hands hold a book
guessing animals' puzzles
written in haiku

Can you guess who from her haiku?

It's YOU!

Haiku is a style of Japanese poetry. The *hai* in *haiku* means "to make light of" or "to make a joke of." So traditional haiku have an element of play. The haiku in this book also have a sense of play. For example, try covering the middle line of this poem and just reading the first and last lines:

a chunk of swiss cheese
chewing sounds heard from a hole
in the kitchen wall

Is the cheese in the wall? Yes! It is in the tummy of the mouse, who is in the wall. Isn't that silly? Try covering the middle line of other haiku in this book.

Traditionally, haiku are three lines long. The first line has five syllables. The second line has seven syllables. The third line has five syllables again.

What's a syllable? It's a small part of a word. To find the syllables in a word, try this: Put your hand under your chin and say "hello." How many times did your chin drop? It should have dropped two times, because *hello* has two syllables: *hel-lo*. Try it with the lines of poetry in this book.

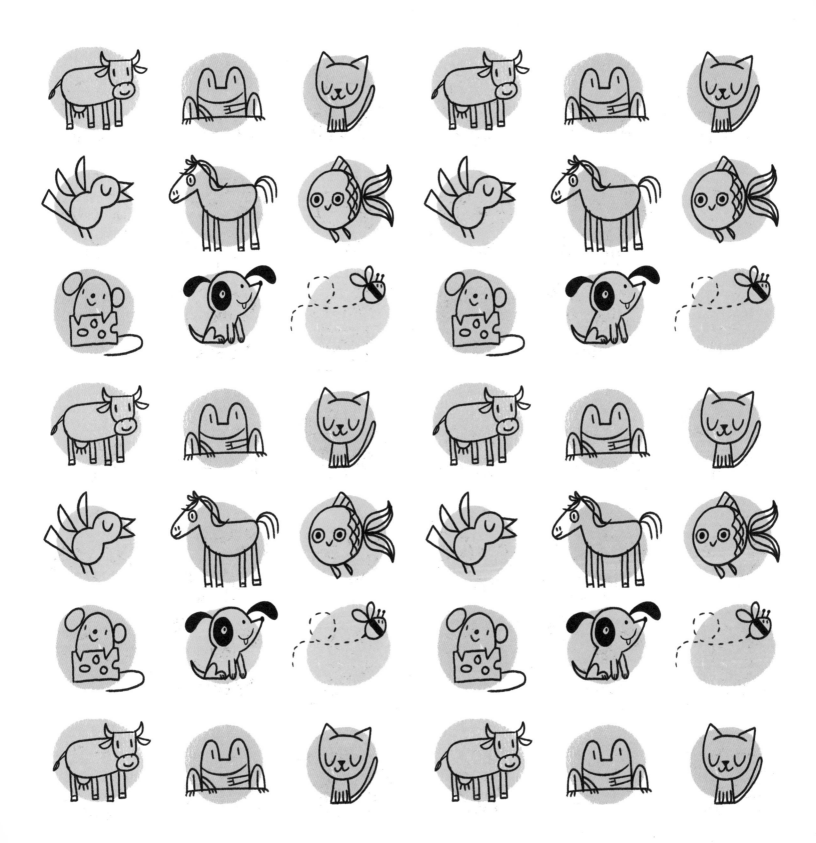